Twelve
Dancing Princesses

Written by Geraldine McCaughrean

Illustrated by Bee Willey

OXFORD
UNIVERSITY PRESS

Chapter 1

Holey boots

Tramper could feel the stony road through the holes in his boots. A newspaper blew by, Tramper picked it up and sat down to cover the holes in his boots with the paper.

A frail old lady glared and stared at him.

"You think you have shoe troubles!" she said. "The King has twelve girls and all of them have holes in their slippers!"

The old lady's feet were bare, cut and purple with cold.
Tramper felt sorry for her, so he gave her his shabby boots.
To thank him, she gave Tramper her dirty cloak. As she clumped
away down the road, she called:

"Stay awake.

Drink no drop.

Sip no sup.

Taste no cup."

"An odd way to say goodbye," thought Tramper.

Chapter 2

The mystery

Rain drizzled down. Tramper put on the cloak and tried to read what was left of the wet newspaper. As it fell apart in his hands he read:

PALACE NOTICE

WANTED:
Answer to the Mystery of the Worn Slippers.

REWARD:
Princess' hand in marriage.

SNAG:
All those who fail will be locked up.

"Why not?" thought Tramper. "I bet I could solve the mystery. I've got nothing to lose, I don't even have any boots." And, when he looked down, his feet were gone too. His feet, legs and body had gone. He was invisible. "The cloak is magic!" he gasped.

The King's twelve daughters were a mystery. Each night they slipped off their silk slippers and went to bed. But each morning their silk slippers were full of holes, and the girls were worn out.

How could it happen? The girls' bedroom door was locked, so they could not get out.

How could it go on? The King was spending all his money on slippers!

Princes came from everywhere to solve the mystery. Each stood watching the princesses as they slept. Each tried to keep awake by choosing which one of the princesses he would marry. But the next morning he woke up on the couch, surrounded by sleeping princesses and twenty-four holey slippers. And after the third time, the royal guard threw him into prison.

Princes stopped coming and knights came instead, then squires. They were all determined to solve the mystery, but they all failed.

The King was furious. New slippers had to be bought every day. The prisons were full to bursting with princes, knights and squires. But Tramper didn't know any of this.

Tramper went to the castle and stood before the King.
"You have no boots!" said the King in deep disgust.
"And you keep running out of slippers," said Tramper.

Chapter 3

Sleeping princesses

The princesses were kind to Tramper. "A brave man deserves a good supper," they said, and brought him baked salmon and a glass of milk. He ate the salmon but remembering the advice of the old lady, he did not drink one drop of milk. Secretly, he let the cat drink the milk, until, with a miaow, it fell off the window sill, sound asleep.

"So that's the trick!" thought Tramper.

The princesses went to bed and Tramper lay down on the couch. He snored loudly, pretending to sleep.

Later that night ... the distant sound of a strange music began. The princesses jumped out of bed and slipped their feet into their brand new slippers. Then they all climbed into the wardrobe!

Chapter 4

The magical wardrobe

The princesses pushed between the hanging clothes and ran down a passageway. Tramper followed them with the old lady's magic cloak over his head. The princesses ran across a garden of ruby roses, through an orchard of diamond fruit and up some glass steps towards a magnificent castle. Tramper ran after them.

The princesses twirled into a great hall. There, waiting for them were twelve shadowy shapes. Twelve elves. Tramper watched as they danced. The elves' shoes were hard, but the soles of the silken slippers were soon worn thin.

"So that's the trick!" said Tramper.

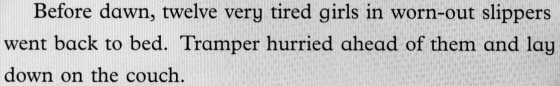

Before dawn, twelve very tired girls in worn-out slippers went back to bed. Tramper hurried ahead of them and lay down on the couch.

There the King found him, surrounded by tattered slippers, snoring loudly. "Well?"

You might think that Tramper told the King about what he had seen, but no. He had enjoyed the salmon so much that he was hoping for a second supper.

"Two more tries," said the King. "That's all!"

Chapter 5

Two more tries

 The next night, the princesses brought Tramper turkey and a cup of tea for his supper. He gobbled down the turkey but *sipped no sup*. He gave the palace parrot his tea and it fell off its perch, sound asleep.

The princesses and
Tramper fell asleep, too –
or so it seemed.

Later that night … the distant sound of silvery music began.
The twelve princesses jumped out of bed, into the wardrobe,
and ran across the garden of ruby roses, through the orchard
of diamond fruit and up the glass steps into the castle. Tramper
followed them with the magic cloak over his head.

Again the elves were waiting. Again the princesses danced and danced until their slippers were ragged.

Before dawn, the princesses made their weary way home. Tramper hurried ahead of them and lay down on the couch.

There the King found him, surrounded by tattered slippers, snoring loudly. "Well?"

You might think that Tramper told the King about what he had seen, but no. He had enjoyed the turkey so much that he was hoping for a third supper.

"One more night," said the King, "… and what's wrong with the parrot?"

The next night, the princesses brought him chicken pie and a glass of water. He swallowed down the pie but he did not drink or sip or even taste the water.

He poured the water into a vase and the roses drooped their sleepy heads.

Again, the princesses slept, or so it seemed, until the distant sound of shimmering music began once again. They climbed out of their beds, into their slippers and through the wardrobe.

They ran across the garden of ruby roses, through the orchard of diamond fruit, and up the castle steps.

In the castle hall, the twelve elves were waiting for the princesses, who danced until the fire burned out and the soles of their slippers were worn to tatters.

Even Tramper joined in.

"Your time is up," said the King the next morning, when he found Tramper asleep on the couch. Two dozen slippers lay, worn out, around him.

Do you think Tramper put on his magic cloak and ran? No. Do you think he told the unbelievable truth? He did.

"I followed your daughters through their wardrobe, into a garden of ruby roses and an orchard of diamond fruit, to a castle of magical elves where they danced and danced until the soles of their slippers wore thin."

"Liar!" said the princesses.

"Rubbish!" said the King.

"I can prove it," said Tramper and put his hand into his pocket and pulled out one ruby rose and one diamond pear. "Shall I nail the wardrobe shut, Your Majesty, before your daughters are danced away?"

"Clever man!" roared the King. "Marry my oldest daughter! Then one day you will be king!"

But Tramper chose the youngest, because she was the best dancer.

There was lots of dancing at the wedding, all of it barefoot. Then everyone put on their silken shoes and went home, as happy as can be.

Once upon a time...

The end.